T4-ADP-258

The Short Fiction of Nella Larsen

©2010 Wilder Publications

All rights reserved. Printed in the United States of America. No part of this book may be used or reproduced in any manner without written permission except for brief quotations for review purposes only.

Wilder Publications, Inc.
PO Box 243
Blacksburg, VA 24060-0243

ISBN 10: 1-60459-991-X
ISBN 13: 978-1-60459-991-6
First Edition

10 9 8 7 6 5 4 3 2 1

The Short Fiction of Nella Larsen

By Nella Larsen

Contents

"Freedom". 187
"The Wrong Man". 191
"Sanctuary"................................... 196

Freedom

He wondered, as he walked deftly through the impassioned traffic on the Avenue, how she would adjust her life if he were to withdraw from it.... How peaceful it would be to have no woman in one's life! These months away took on the appearance of a liberation, a temporary recess from a hateful existence in which he lived in intimacy with someone he did not know and would not now have chosen.... He began, again, to speculate on the pattern her life would take without him. Abruptly, it flashed upon him that the vague irritation of many weeks was a feeling of smoldering resentment against her. The displeasure that this realization caused him increased his ill humor and distaste. He began to dissect her with an acrimony that astonished himself. Her unanimated beauty seemed now only a thin disguise for an inert mind, and not for the serene beauty of soul which he had attributed to her. He suspected, too, a touch of depravity, perhaps only physical, but more likely mental as well. Reflection convinced him that her appeal for him was bounded by the senses, for witness his disgust and clarity of vision, now that they were separated. How could he have been so blinded? Why, for him she had been the universe; a universe personal and unheedful of outside persons or things. He had adored her in a slavish fashion. He groaned inwardly at his own mental caricature of himself, sitting dumb, staring at her in fatuous worship. What an ass he had been!

His work here was done, but what was there to prevent him from staying away for six months—a year—forever? ... Never to see her again! ... He stopped, irresolute. What would she do? He tried to construct a representation of her future without him. In his present new hatred, she became a creature irresistibly given to pleasure at no matter what cost. A sybarite! A parasite too!

He was prayerfully thankful that appreciation of his danger had come before she had sapped from him all physical and spiritual vitality. But her future troubled him even while he assured himself that he knew its road, and laughed ruefully at the picture of her flitting from mate to mate.

A feverish impatience gripped him. Somehow, he must contrive to get himself out of the slough into which his amorous folly had precipitated him. ... Three years. Good God! At the moment, those three years seemed the most precious of his life. And he had foolishly thrown them away. He had drifted pleasantly, peacefully, without landmarks; would be drifting yet but for the death of a friend whose final affairs had brought him away....

He started. Death! Perhaps she would die. How that would simplify matters for him. But no; she would not die. He laughed without amusement. She would not die; she would outlast him, damn her! ... An angry resentment, sharp and painful as a whiplash, struck him. Its passing left him calm and determined....

He braced himself and continued to walk. He had decided; he would stay. With this decision, he seemed to be reborn. He felt cool, refreshed, as if he had stepped out from a warm, scented place into a cold, brisk breeze. He was happy. The world had turned to silver and gold, and life again became a magical adventure. Even the placards in the shops shone with the light of paradise upon them. One caught and held his eye. Travel.. . Yes, he would travel; lose himself in India, China, the South Seas ... Radiance from the most battered vehicle and the meanest pedestrian. Gladness flooded him. He was free.

A year, thick with various adventures, had slid by since that spring day on which he had wrenched himself free. He had lived, been happy, and with no woman in his life. The break had been simple: a telegram hinting at prolonged business and indefinite return. There had been no reply. This had annoyed him, but he told himself it was what he had expected. He would not admit that, perhaps, he had missed her letter in his wanderings. He had persuaded himself to believe what he wanted to believe—that she had not cared. Actually, there had been confusion in his mind, a complex of thoughts which made it difficult to know what he really had thought. He had imagined that he shuddered at the idea that she had accepted the most generous offer. He pitied her. There was, too, a touch of sadness, a sense of something lost, which he irritably explained on the score of her beauty. Beauty of any kind always stirred him.... Too bad a woman like that couldn't be decent. He was well rid of her.

But what had she done? How had he taken it? His contemptuous mood visualized her at times, laughing merrily at some jest made by his successor, or again sitting silent, staring into the fire. He would be conscious of every detail of her appearance: her hair simply arranged, her soft dark eyes, her delicate chin propped on hands rivaling the perfection of La

Gioconda's. Sometimes there would be a reversion to the emotions which had ensnared him, when he ached with yearning, when he longed for her again. Such moments were rare.

Another year passed, during which his life had widened, risen, and then crashed....

Dead? How could she be dead? Dead in childbirth, they had told him, both his mistress and the child she had borne him. She had been dead on that spring day when, resentful and angry at her influence in his life, he had reached out toward freedom—to find only a mirage; for he saw quite plainly that now he would never be free. It was she who had escaped him. Each time he had cursed and wondered, it had been a dead woman whom he had cursed and about whom he had wondered.... He shivered; he seemed always to be cold now.....

Well rid of her! How well he had not known, nor how easily. She was dead. And he had cursed her. But one didn't curse the dead.... Didn't one? Damn her! Why couldn't she have lived, or why hadn't she died sooner? For long months he had wondered how she had arranged her life, and all the while she had done nothing but to complete it by dying.

The futility of all his speculations exasperated him. His old resentment returned. She *had* spoiled his life; first by living and then by dying. He hated the fact that she had finished with him, rather than he with her. He could not forgive her.... Forgive her? She was dead. He felt somehow that, after all, the dead did not care if you forgave them or not.

Gradually, his mind became puppet to a disturbing tension which drove it back and forth between two thoughts: he had left her; she was dead. These two facts became lodged in his mind like burrs pricking at his breaking faculties. As he recalled the manner of his leaving her, it seemed increasingly brutal. She had died loving him, bearing him a child, and he had left her. He tried to shake off the heavy mental dejection which weighed him down, but his former will and determination deserted him. The vitality of the past, forever dragging him down into black depression, frightened him. The mental fog, thick as soot, into which the news of her death had trapped him, appalled him. He must get himself out. A wild anger seized him. He began to think of his own death, self-inflicted, with feeling that defied analysis. His zest for life became swallowed up in the rising tide of sorrow and mental chaos which was engulfing him.

As autumn approached, with faint notice on his part, his anger and resentment retreated, leaving in their wake a gentle stir of regret and remorse.

Imperceptibly, he grew physically weary; a strange sensation of loneliness and isolation enveloped him. A species of timidity came upon him; he felt an unhappy remoteness from people, and began to edge away from life.

His deepening sense of isolation drove him more and more back upon his memories. Sunk in his armchair before the fire, he passed the days and sometimes the nights, for he had lost count of these, merged as they were into one another.

His increasing mental haziness had rejected the fact of her death; often she was there with him, just beyond the firelight or the candlelight. She talked and laughed with him. Sometimes, at night, he woke to see her standing over him or sitting in his chair before the dying fire. By some mysterious process, the glory of first love flamed again in him. He forgot that they had ever parted. His twisted memories visioned her with him in places where she had never been. He had forgotten all but the past, and that was brightly distorted.

He sat waiting for her. He seemed to remember that she had promised to come. Outside, the street was quiet. She was late. Why didn't she come? Childish tears fell over his cold cheeks. He sat weeping in front of the sinking fire.

A nameless dread seized him; she would not come! In the agony of his disappointment, he did not see that the fire had died and the candles had sputtered out. He sat wrapped in immeasurable sadness. He knew that she would not come.

Something in this thought fired his disintegrating brain. She would not come; then he must go to her.

He rose, shaking with cold, and groped toward the door. Yes, he would go to her.

The gleam of a streetlight through a French window caught his attention. He stumbled toward it. His cold fingers fumbled a moment with the catch, but he tore it open with a spark of his old determination and power, and stepped out—and down to the pavement a hundred feet below.

The Wrong Man

The room blazed with color. It seemed that the gorgeous things which the women were wearing had for this once managed to subdue the strident tones of the inevitable black and white of the men's costumes. Tonight they lent just enough of preciseness to add interest to the riotously hued scene. The place was crowded but cool, for a gentle breeze blew from the Sound through the large open windows and doors, now and then stirring some group of flowers.

Julia Romley, in spite of the smoke-colored chiffon gown (ordered specially for the occasion) which she was wearing, seemed even more flamingly clad than the rest. The pale indefinite gray but increased the flaring mop of her hair; scarlet, a poet had called it. The satiny texture of her skin seemed also to reflect in her cheeks a cozy tinge of that red mass.

Julia, however, was not happy tonight. A close observer would have said that she was actively disturbed. Faint abstraction, trite remarks nervously offered, and uncontrolled restlessness marred her customary perfect composure. Her dreamy gray eyes stole frequently in the direction of Myra Redmon's party. Myra always had a lion in tow, but why that particular man? She shook a little as she wondered.

Suddenly, the orchestra blared into something wild and impressionistic, with a primitive staccato understrain of jazz. The buzz of conversation died, strangled by the savage strains of the music. The crowd stirred, broke, coalesced into twos, and became a whirling mass. A partner claimed Julia and they became part of the swaying mob.

"Some show, what?" George Hill's drawling voice was saying, while he secretly wondered what had got into Julia; she was so quiet, not like herself at all.

Julia let her eyes wander over the moving crowd. Young men, old men, young women, older women, slim girls, fat women, thin men, stout men, glided by. The old nursery rhyme came into her mind. She repeated it to George in a singsong tone:

"Rich man, poor man,
Beggar man, thief,
Doctor, lawyer,
Indian chief."

George nodded. "Yes, that's it. Everybody's here and a few more. And look, look! There's the 'Indian chief.' Wonder who he is? He certainly looks the part."

Julia didn't look; she knew what she would see. A tall, thin man, his lean face yellowed and hardened as if by years in the tropics; a man, perhaps, a bit unused to scenes of this kind, purposely a little aloof and, one suspected, more than a little contemptuous.

She felt a flash of resentful anger against Myra. Why was she always carting about impossible people? It was disgusting. It was worse— it was dangerous. Certainly it was about to become dangerous to her, Julia Romley, erstwhile . ... She let the thought die unfinished, it was too unpleasant.

She had been so happy, so secure, and now this: Ralph Tyler, risen from the past to shatter the happiness which she had grasped for herself. Must she begin all over again? She made a hasty review of her life since San Francisco days: Chicago and the art school where she had studied interior decorating with the money that Ralph Tyler had given her; New York, her studio and success; Boston, and marriage to Jim Romley. And now this envied gay life in one of Long Island's most exclusive sets. Yes, life had been good to her at last, better than she had ever dreamed. Was she about to lose everything—love, wealth, and position? She shivered.

"Cold?" Again George's drawling voice dragging her back to the uncertain present.

"No, not cold. Just someone walking over my grave," she answered laughingly. "I'm rotten company tonight, George. I'm sorry; I'll do better. It's the crowd, I guess."

Her husband claimed her for the next dance. A happy married pair, their obvious joy in each other after five wedded years was the subject of amused comment and mild jokes among their friends. "The everlasting lovers," they were dubbed, and the name suited them as perfectly as they suited each other.

"What's wrong, Julie, old girl?" asked Jim after a few minutes' baffled scrutiny. "Tired?"

"Nothing, nothing. I just feel small, so futile in this crush; sort of trapped, you know. Why *do* the Arnolds have so many people to their things?" Quickly regretting her display of irritation, she added: "It's wonderful, though—the people, the music, the color, and these lovely rooms, like a princess's ball in a fairy tale."

"Yes, great," he agreed. "Lots of strangers here, too; most of them distinguished people from town."

"Who's the tall browned man with Myra, who looks like—well, like an Indian chief?" She laughed a little at her own pleasantry, just to show Jim that there was nothing troubling her.

"Doesn't he, though? Sort of self-sufficient and superior and a bit indifferent, as if he owned us all and despised the whole tribe of us. I guess you can't blame him much. He probably thinks we're a soft, lazy, self-pampering lot. He's Ralph Tyler, an explorer, just back from some godforsaken place on the edge of nowhere. Been head of some expedition lost somewhere in Asia for years, given up for dead. Discovered a buried city or something; great contribution to civilization and all that, you know. They say he brought back some emeralds worth a king's ransom."

"Do you know him, Jim?"

"Yes; knew him years ago in college. Didn't think he'd remember me after such a long time and all those thrilling adventures, but he did. Honestly, you could have knocked me over with a feather when he came over to me and put out his hand and said, 'Hello there, Jim Romley.' Nice, wasn't it?" Jim's handsome face glowed. He was undoubtedly flattered by the great man's remembrance. He went on enthusiastically: "I'm going to have him out to the house, Julie; that is, if I can get him. Small, handpicked dinner party. What say?"

She shivered again.

"Cold?"

"No, not cold. Just someone walking over my grave." She laughed, amused at the double duty of the superstition in one evening, and glad too that Jim had not noticed that his question had passed unanswered.

Dance followed dance. She wasn't being a success tonight. She knew it, but somehow she couldn't make small talk. Her thoughts kept wandering to that tall browned man who had just come back from the world's end. One or two of her partners, after trying in vain to draw her out, looked at her quizzically, wondering if the impossible had happened. Had Julia and old Jim quarreled?

At last she escaped to a small deserted room on an upper floor, where she could be alone to think. She groped about in her mind for some way to avoid that dinner party. It spelled disaster. She must find some way to keep Ralph Tyler from finding out that she was the wife of his old schoolmate. But if he were going to be here for any length of time, and Jim seemed to think that he would, she would have to meet him. Perhaps she could go away? ... No, she dared not; anything might happen. Better to be on hand to ward off the blow when it fell. She sighed, suddenly weary and beaten. It was hopeless. And she had been so happy! Just a faint shadow of uneasiness, at first, which had gradually faded as the years slipped away.

She sat for a long time in deep thought. Her face settled into determined lines; she made up her mind. She would ask, plead if necessary, for his silence. It was the only way. It would be hard, humiliating even, but it must be done if she were to continue to be happy in Jim's love. She couldn't bear to look ahead to years without him.

She crossed the room and wrote a note to Ralph Tyler, asking him to meet her in the summerhouse in one of the gardens. She hesitated a moment over the signature, finally writing *Julia Hammond,* in order to prepare him a little for the meeting.

After she had given the note into the hand of a servant for delivery "to Mr. Tyler, the man with Mrs. Redmon," she experienced a slight feeling of relief. "At least I can try," she thought as she made her way to the summerhouse to wait. "Surely, if I tell him about myself and Jim, he'll be merciful."

The man looked curiously at the woman sitting so motionless in the summerhouse in the rock garden. Even in the darkness she felt his gaze upon her, though she lacked the courage to raise her eyes to look at him. She waited expectantly for him to speak.

After what seemed hours but was, she knew, only seconds, she understood that he was waiting for her to break the silence. So she began to speak in a low hesitating voice:

"I suppose you think it strange, this request of mine to meet me here alone; but I had to see you, to talk to you. I wanted to tell you about my marriage to Jim Romley. You know him?"

"Yes, I know him."

"Well," she went on, eagerly now, "you see, we're so happy! Jim's so splendid, and I've tried to be such a good wife. And I thought— I thought—you see, I thought—" The eager voice trailed off on a note of entreaty.

"Yes, you thought?" prompted the man in a noncommittal tone.

"Well, you see, I thought that if you knew how happy we were, and how much I love him, and that since you know Jim, that you— you—"

She stopped. She couldn't go on, she simply couldn't. But she must. There he stood like a long, menacing shadow between her and the future. She began again, this time with insinuating flattery:

"You have so much yourself now—honor, fame, and money—and you've done such splendid things! You've suffered too. How you must have suffered! Oh, I'm glad of your success; you deserve it. You're a hero, a great man. A little thing like that can't matter to you now and it means everything to me, everything. Please spare me my little happiness. Please be kind!"

"But I don't understand." The man's voice was puzzled. "How 'kind'? What is it you're asking?"

Reading masked denial in the question, Julia began to sob softly.

"Don't tell Jim! Please, don't tell Jim! I'll do anything to keep him from knowing, anything."

"But aren't you making a mistake? I—"

"Mistake?" She laughed bitterly. "I see; you think I should have told him. You think that even now I should tell him that I was your mistress once. You don't know Jim. He'd never forgive that. He wouldn't understand that, when a girl has been sick and starving on the streets, anything can happen to her; that she's grateful for food and shelter at any price. You won't tell him, will you?"

"But I'm sure," stammered the tall figure, fumbling for cigarettes, "I'm sure you've made a mistake. I'm sorry. I've been trying to—"

Julia cut him off. She couldn't bear to hear him speak the refusing words, his voice seemed so grimly final. She knew it was useless, but she made a last desperate effort:

"I was so young, so foolish, and so hungry; but Jim wouldn't understand." She choked over the last words.

He shook his head—impatiently, it seemed to the agonized woman.

"Mrs. Romley, I've been trying to tell you that you've made a mistake. I'm sorry. However, I can assure you that your secret is safe with me. It will never be from my lips that Jim Romley hears you have been—er—what you say you have been."

Only the woman's sharply drawn quivering breath indicated that she had heard. A match blazed for a moment as he lighted his cigarette with shaking hands. Julia's frightened eyes picked out his face in the flickering light. She uttered a faint dismayed cry.

She had told the wrong man.

Sanctuary

1

On the Southern coast, between Merton and Shawboro, there is a strip of desolation some half a mile wide and nearly ten miles long between the sea and old fields of ruined plantations. Skirting the edge of this narrow jungle is a partly grown-over road which still shows traces of furrows made by the wheels of wagons that have long since rotted away or been cut into firewood. This road is little used, now that the state has built its new highway a bit to the west and wagons are less numerous than automobiles.

In the forsaken road a man was walking swiftly. But in spite of his hurry, at every step he set down his feet with infinite care, for the night was windless and the heavy silence intensified each sound; even the breaking of a twig could be plainly heard. And the man had need of caution as well as haste.

Before a lonely cottage that shrank timidly back from the road the man hesitated a moment, then struck out across the patch of green in front of it. Stepping behind a clump of bushes close to the house, he looked in through the lighted window at Annie Poole, standing at her kitchen table mixing the supper biscuits.

He was a big, black man with pale brown eyes in which there was an odd mixture of fear and amazement. The light showed streaks of gray soil on his heavy, sweating face and great hands, and on his torn clothes. In his woolly hair clung bits of dried leaves and dead grass.

He made a gesture as if to tap on the window, but turned away to the door instead. Without knocking he opened it and went in.

2

The woman's brown gaze was immediately on him, though she did not move. She said, "You ain't in no hurry, is you, Jim Hammer?" It wasn't, however, entirely a question.

"Ah's in trubble, Mis' Poole," the man explained, his voice shaking, his fingers twitching.

"W'at you done done now?"

"Shot a man, Mis' Poole."

"Trufe?" The woman seemed calm. But the word was spat out.

"Yas'm. Shot 'im." In the man's tone was something of wonder, as if he himself could not quite believe that he had really done this thing which he affirmed.

"Daid?"

"Dunno, Mis' Poole. Dunno."

"White man o' niggah?"

"Cain't say, Mis' Poole. White man, Ah reckons."

Annie Poole looked at him with cold contempt. She was a tiny, withered woman—fifty perhaps—with a wrinkled face the color of old copper, framed by a crinkly mass of white hair. But about her small figure was some quality of hardness that belied her appearance of frailty. At last she spoke, boring her sharp little eyes into those of the anxious creature before her.

"An' w'at am you lookin' foh me to do 'bout et?"

"Jes' lemme stop till dey's gone by. Hide me till dey passes. Reckon dey ain't fur off now." His begging voice changed to a frightened whimper. "Foh de Lawd's sake, Mis' Poole, lemme stop."

And why, the woman inquired caustically, should she run the dangerous risk of hiding him?

"Obadiah, he'd lemme stop ef he was to home," the man whined.

Annie Poole sighed. "Yas," she admitted slowly, reluctantly, "Ah spec' he would. Obadiah, he's too good to youall no 'count trash." Her slight shoulders lifted in a hopeless shrug. "Yas, Ah reckon he'd do et. Emspecial' seein' how he allus set such a heap o' store by you. Cain't see w'at foh, mahse'f. Ah shuah don' see nuffin' in you but a heap o'dirt."

But a look of irony, of cunning, of complicity passed over her face. She went on, "Still, 'siderin' all an' all, how Obadiah's right fon' o' you, an' how white folks is white folks, Ah'm a-gwine hide you dis one time."

Crossing the kitchen, she opened a door leading into a small bedroom, saying, "Git yo'se'f in dat dere feather baid an' Ah'm a-gwine put de clo's on de top. Don' reckon dey'll fin' you ef dey does look foh you in mah house. An Ah don' spec' dey'll go foh to do dat. Not lessen you been keerless an' let 'em smell you out gittin' hyah." She turned on him a withering look. "But you allus been triflin'. Cain't do nuffin' propah. An' Ah'm a-tellin' you ef dey warn't white folks an' you a po' niggah, Ah shuah wouldn't be lettin' you mess up mah feather baid dis ebenin', 'cose Ah jes' plain don' want you hyah. Ah done kep' mahse'f outen trubble all mah life. So's Obadiah."

"Ah's powahful 'bliged to you, Mis' Poole. You shuah am one good 'oman. De Lawd'll mos' suttinly—"

Annie Poole cut him off. "Dis ain't no time foh all dat kin' o' fiddle-de-roll. Ah does mah duty as Ah sees et 'thout no thanks from you. Ef de Lawd had gib you a white face 'stead o' dat dere black one, Ah shuah would turn you out. Now hush yo' mouf an' git yo'se'f in. An' don' git movin' and scrunchin' undah dose covahs and git yo'se'f kotched in mah house."

Without further comment the man did as he was told. After he had laid his soiled body and grimy garments between her snowy sheets, Annie Poole carefully rearranged the covering and placed piles of freshly laundered linen on top. Then she gave a pat here and there, eyed the result, and, finding it satisfactory, went back to her cooking.

3

Jim Hammer settled down to the racking business of waiting until the approaching danger should have passed him by. Soon savory odors seeped in to him and he realized that he was hungry. He wished that Annie Poole would bring him something to eat. Just one biscuit. But she wouldn't, he knew. Not she. She was a hard one, Obadiah's mother.

By and by he fell into a sleep from which he was dragged back by the rumbling sound of wheels in the road outside. For a second fear clutched so tightly at him that he almost leaped from the suffocating shelter of the bed in order to make some active attempt to escape the horror that his capture meant. There was a spasm at his heart, a pain so sharp, so slashing, that he had to suppress an impulse to cry out. He felt himself falling. Down, down, down ... Everything grew dim and very distant in his memory.... Vanished ... Came rushing back.

Outside there was silence. He strained his ears. Nothing. No footsteps. No voices. They had gone on then. Gone without even stopping to ask Annie Poole if she had seen him pass that way. A sigh of relief slipped from him. His thick lips curled in an ugly, cunning smile. It had been smart of him to think of coming to Obadiah's mother's to hide. She was an old demon, but he was safe in her house.

He lay a short while longer, listening intently, and, hearing nothing, started to get up. But immediately he stopped, his yellow eyes glowing like pale flames. He had heard the unmistakable sound of men coming toward the house. Swiftly he slid back into the heavy, hot stuffiness of the bed and lay listening fearfully.

The terrifying sounds drew nearer. Slowly. Heavily. Just for a moment he thought they were not coming in—they took so long. But there was a light knock and the noise of a door being opened. His whole body went taut. His feet felt frozen, his hands clammy, his tongue like a weighted, dying thing. His pounding heart made it hard for his straining ears to hear what they were saying out there.

"Ebenin', Mistah Lowndes." Annie Poole's voice sounded as it always did, sharp and dry.

There was no answer. Or had he missed it? With slow care he shifted his position, bringing his head nearer the edge of the bed. Still he heard nothing. What were they waiting for? Why didn't they ask about him?

Annie Poole, it seemed, was of the same mind. "Ah don' reckon youall done traipsed way out hyah jes' foh yo' healf," she hinted.

"There's bad news for you, Annie, I'm 'fraid." The sheriff's voice was low and queer.

Jim Hammer visualized him standing out there—a tall, stooped man, his white tobacco-stained mustache drooping limply at the ends, his nose hooked and sharp, his eyes blue and cold. Bill Lowndes was a hard one too. And white.

"W'atall bad news, Mistah Lowndes?" The woman put the question quietly, directly.

"Obadiah—" the sheriff began—hesitated—began again. "Obadiah—ah—er
—he's outside, Annie. I'm 'fraid—"

"Shucks! You done missed. Obadiah, he ain't done nuffin', Mistah Lowndes. Obadiah!" she called stridently, "Obadiah! git hyah an' splain yo'se'f."

But Obadiah didn't answer, didn't come in. Other men came in. Came in with steps that dragged and halted. No one spoke. Not even Annie Poole. Something was laid carefully upon the floor.

"Obadiah, chile," his mother said softly, "Obadiah, chile." Then, with sudden alarm, "He ain't daid, is he? Mistah Lowndes! Obadiah, he ain't daid?"

Jim Hammer didn't catch the answer to that pleading question. A new fear was stealing over him.

"There was a to-do, Annie," Bill Lowndes explained gently, "at the garage back o' the factory. Fellow tryin' to steal tires. Obadiah heerd a noise an' run out with two or three others. Scared the rascal all right. Fired off his gun an' run. We allow et to be Jim Hammer. Picked up his cap back there. Never was no 'count. Thievin' an' sly. But we'll git 'im, Annie. We'll git 'im."

The man huddled in the feather bed prayed silently. "Oh, Lawd! Ah didn't go to do et. Not Obadiah, Lawd. You knows dat. You knows et."

And into his frenzied brain came the thought that it would be better for him to get up and go out to them before Annie Poole gave him away. For he was lost now. With all his great strength he tried to get himself out of the bed. But he couldn't.

"Oh, Lawd!" he moaned. "Oh, Lawd!" His thoughts were bitter and they ran through his mind like panic. He knew that it had come to pass as it said somewhere in the Bible about the wicked. The Lord had stretched out his hand and smitten him. He was paralyzed. He couldn't move hand or foot. He moaned again. It was all there was left for him to do. For in the terror of this new calamity that had come upon him he had forgotten the waiting danger which was so near out there in the kitchen.

His hunters, however, didn't hear him. Bill Lowndes was saying, "We been a-lookin' for Jim out along the old road. Figured he'd make tracks for Shawboro. You ain't noticed anybody pass this evenin', Annie?"

The reply came promptly, unwaveringly. "No, Ah ain't sees nobody pass. Not yet."

4

Jim Hammer caught his breath.

"Well," the sheriff concluded, "we'll be gittin' along. Obadiah was a mighty fine boy. Ef they was all like him—I'm sorry, Annie. Anything I c'n do, let me know."

"Thank you, Mistah Lowndes."

With the sound of the door closing on the departing men, power to move came back to the man in the bedroom. He pushed his dirt-caked feet out from the covers and rose up, but crouched down again. He wasn't cold now, but hot all over and burning. Almost he wished that Bill Lowndes and his men had taken him with them.

Annie Poole had come into the room.

It seemed a long time before Obadiah's mother spoke. When she did there were no tears, no reproaches; but there was a raging fury in her voice as she lashed out, "Git outer mah feather baid, Jim Hammer, an' outen mah house, an' don' nevah stop thankin' yo' Jesus he done gib you dat black face."